Percy the Park Keeper
A·B·C

NICK BUTTERWORTH

Collins

An Imprint of HarperCollins*Publishers*

First published in Great Britain by HarperCollins Publishers Ltd in 1998

This edition published in 2010

1 3 5 7 9 10 8 6 4 2

ISBN: 978-0-00-786513-0

Visit our website at: www.harpercollins.co.uk

Printed and bound in China

Hello! I'm Percy the Park Keeper!
Would you like to play I-Spy in my
park? It will help you to learn your
A B C, and you can meet all my
animal friends along the way.
Turn the page to start the game.

 I spy something
beginning with a...

They're my friends who live in
the park with me.

animals

I spy something beginning with **b**...

He's black and white – and sometimes he needs a bath!

badger

C c

I spy something
beginning with **c**...

I always wear this when it's cold.

coat

 **D d**   I spy something
beginning with **d** ...

They make a noise like this: QUACK!

ducks

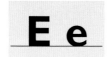

E e

I spy something
beginning with **e**...

This rabbit is my friend.
He is very proud of his long...

ears

F f

I spy something
beginning with **f**...

Lots of these grow in the park in spring.

flowers

G g

I spy something
beginning with **g**...

It's green and we all love lying on it!

grass

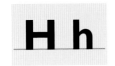

H h

I spy something beginning with **h**...

He's the prickliest animal in the park!

hedgehog

I i

I spy something
beginning with i...

Can you see some of these
hanging from my window?

icicles

J j

I spy something
beginning with j . . .

I think it's time I bought a new one.

jug

K k

I spy something beginning with k...

I use it to make a cup of tea!

kettle

 **L l**

I spy something
beginning with l…

Look at them blowing by!

leaves

M m

I spy something
beginning with **m** . . .

He lives underground - and is
very good at digging!

mole

N n

I spy something
beginning with **n** ...

A mouse is sitting on the end of
the badger's ...

nose

O o

I spy something
beginning with o . . .

o range

P p

I spy something
beginning with p . . .

parcel

Q q

I spy something
beginning with q...

This keeps you nice and warm
in the winter!

quilt

R r

I spy something
beginning with **r**...

This friend of mine
loves jumping.

rabbit

I spy something beginning with s...

I'm looking after him because he's hurt his arm.

squirrel

T t

I spy something
beginning with t...

They often come in handy in the park.

tools

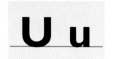

U u

I spy something
beginning with **u**...

They are white with pink spots.
Can you see them on the line?

underpants

V v

I spy something
beginning with **v**...

Flowers look very pretty in this!

vase

Ww

I spy something
beginning with w...

I always have something to
carry in mine.

wheelbarrow

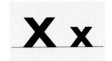

X x

I spy something
ending with x . . .

He's one of my friends and he
lives in the park.

fo**x**

Y y

I spy something
beginning with **y** . . .

I like having this for my lunch!

yoghurt

Z z

I spy something
beginning with z…

I wonder how he came into
the park!

zebra

Here's Percy's alphabet. **A a**

E e   **F f**   **G g**

K k   **L l**   **M m**

Q q   **R r**   **S s**

V v   **W w**   **X x**

Bb Cc Dd

Hh Ii Jj

Nn Oo Pp

Tt Uu

Yy Zz